Let's Go, Patriots!

Aimee Aryal

Illustrated by Miguel De Angel

with Brad Vinson

www.mascotbooks.com

It was a beautiful fall day in New England. Patriots fans from all over the area were making their way to the stadium for a football game.

All over town, everyone dressed in Patriots colors. As fans made their way to the stadium, they cheered, "Let's go, Patriots!"

Hours before the start of the game, Patriots fans began gathering in the parking lot. The smell of good food was in the air as smoke billowed from grills. Some children, and even a few grown-ups, painted their faces for the game!

As fans walked through the
stadium gates, they cheered,
"Let's go, Patriots!"

The team gathered in the locker room before the game. Players strapped on their pads and dressed in their New England Patriots uniforms.

The coach delivered final instructions and encouraged the team to play their best. The coach cheered, "Let's go, Patriots!"

It was now time for the New England Patriots to take the field. The announcer called, "Ladies and gentlemen, please welcome your New England Patriots!" The team sprinted onto the field as they were greeted by their loyal fans. It was very loud in the stadium!

The Patriots huddled around the team captains and cheered, "Let's go, Patriots!"

The team captains met at midfield for the coin toss. The referee flipped a coin high in the air and the visiting team called, "Heads." The coin landed with the heads side up – the Patriots would begin the game by kicking off.

The referee reminded the players that it was important to play hard, but also with good sportsmanship.

The Patriots kicker booted the ball down the field to start the action. With the game underway, the kicker cheered, "Let's go, Patriots!"

After the opening kickoff, it was time for the Patriots defense to take the field. One fan led the crowd in a "DE-FENSE" chant, holding up a "D" in one hand and a picket fence in the other. With the crowd's encouragement, the Patriots defense sacked the quarterback. Fans appreciated the great play and cheered, "Let's go, Patriots!"

After the defense did its job, the Patriots offense went to work. With great teamwork, they marched right down the field. On fourth down, the team was only one yard away from the end zone.

"Let's go for it!" instructed the coach, and the quarterback called a play in the huddle.

The quarterback yelled, "Down. Set. Hike!" before handing the ball to the running back, who crossed the goal line.

TOUCHDOWN!

After the score, the crowd erupted with joy. Fans cheered, "Let's go, Patriots!"

At the end of the first half, the Patriots headed back to the locker room. The coach stopped to answer a few questions from a television reporter. In the locker room, the team rested and prepared for the second half.

Meanwhile, Patriots fans stretched their legs and picked up a few snacks at the concession stands. In the concourse, Patriots fans cheered, "Let's go, Patriots!"

In the second half, the temperature dropped and snow began to fall. The team played hard through the blizzard. Young Patriots fans drank hot chocolate to help them stay warm. One little fan was surprised to see herself on the big screen. With everybody watching, she cheered, "Let's go, Patriots!"

With only a few seconds remaining, the score was tied. The Patriots lined-up for a field goal try. After a good snap and a perfect hold, the kicker booted the ball toward the goal posts. The stadium was nearly silent as all eyes followed the flight of the ball.

The kick was good!

The New England Patriots won the football game! The kicker cheered, "Let's go, Patriots!"

To celebrate the thrilling victory, Patriots players dumped water on the coach. The teams shook hands and congratulated each other on a good game. As Patriots fans left the stadium, they cheered, "Let's go, Patriots!"

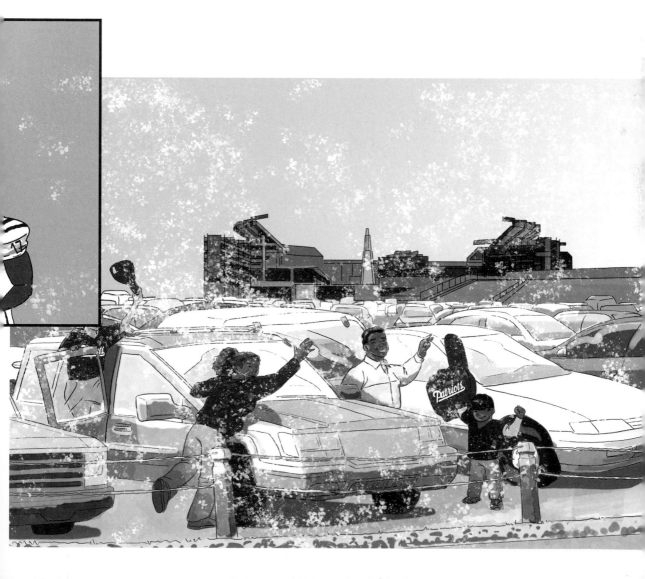

For Anna and Maya. ~ Aimee Aryal

For Sue, Ana Milagros, and Angel Miguel. ~ Miguel De Angel

New England Patriots Charitable Foundation

The New England Patriots Charitable Foundation was established in 1994 by the Kraft family to support charitable and philanthropic agencies throughout New England. This support comes in the form of direct grants, and the donation of signed memorabilia to a variety of charitable causes, and from Patriots players who offer their direct support by appearing at charity functions throughout the year. The Foundation's primary goal is to support programs that aid the youth and families of New England while underscoring the Kraft family's deep commitment to philanthropic activities in the community. For more information about the New England Patriots Charitable Foundation, please visit www.patriots.com/community.

For more information about our products, please visit us online at www.mascotbooks.com.

For more information, please contact Mascot Books,
P.O. Box 220157, Chantilly, VA 20153-0157

ISBN: 978-1-932888-98-0

Printed in the United States.

www.mascotbooks.com

Title List

Team	Book Title	Author	Team	Book Title	Author
Baseball			**Pro Football**		
Boston Red Sox	Hello, Wally!	Jerry Remy	Carolina Panthers	Let's Go, Panthers!	Aimee Aryal
Boston Red Sox	Wally And His Journey Through Red Sox Nation!	Jerry Remy	Dallas Cowboys	How 'Bout Them Cowboys!	Aimee Aryal
			Green Bay Packers	Go, Pack, Go!	Aimee Aryal
New York Yankees	Let's Go, Yankees!	Yogi Berra	Kansas City Chiefs	Let's Go, Chiefs!	Aimee Aryal
New York Mets	Hello, Mr. Met!	Rusty Staub	Minnesota Vikings	Let's Go, Vikings!	Aimee Aryal
St. Louis Cardinals	Hello, Fredbird!	Ozzie Smith	New York Giants	Let's Go, Giants!	Aimee Aryal
Philadelphia Phillies	Hello, Phillie Phanatic!	Aimee Aryal	New England Patriots	Let's Go, Patriots!	Aimee Aryal
Chicago Cubs	Let's Go, Cubs!	Aimee Aryal	Seattle Seahawks	Let's Go, Seahawks!	Aimee Aryal
Chicago White Sox	Let's Go, White Sox!	Aimee Aryal	Washington Redskins	Hail To The Redskins!	Aimee Aryal
Cleveland Indians	Hello, Slider!	Bob Feller			
			Coloring Book		
			Dallas Cowboys	How 'Bout Them Cowboys!	Aimee Aryal
College					
Alabama	Hello, Big Al!	Aimee Aryal	Michigan State	Hello, Sparty!	Aimee Aryal
Alabama	Roll Tide!	Ken Stabler	Minnesota	Hello, Goldy!	Aimee Aryal
Arizona	Hello, Wilbur!	Lute Olson	Mississippi	Hello, Colonel Rebel!	Aimee Aryal
Arkansas	Hello, Big Red!	Aimee Aryal	Mississippi State	Hello, Bully!	Aimee Aryal
Auburn	Hello, Aubie!	Aimee Aryal	Missouri	Hello, Truman!	Todd Donoho
Auburn	War Eagle!	Pat Dye	Nebraska	Hello, Herbie Husker!	Aimee Aryal
Boston College	Hello, Baldwin!	Aimee Aryal	North Carolina	Hello, Rameses!	Aimee Aryal
Brigham Young	Hello, Cosmo!	LaVell Edwards	North Carolina St.	Hello, Mr. Wuf!	Aimee Aryal
Clemson	Hello, Tiger!	Aimee Aryal	Notre Dame	Let's Go, Irish!	Aimee Aryal
Colorado	Hello, Ralphie!	Aimee Aryal	Ohio State	Hello, Brutus!	Aimee Aryal
Connecticut	Hello, Jonathan!	Aimee Aryal	Oklahoma	Let's Go, Sooners!	Aimee Aryal
Duke	Hello, Blue Devil!	Aimee Aryal	Oklahoma State	Hello, Pistol Pete!	Aimee Aryal
Florida	Hello, Albert!	Aimee Aryal	Penn State	Hello, Nittany Lion!	Aimee Aryal
Florida State	Let's Go, 'Noles!	Aimee Aryal	Penn State	We Are Penn State!	Joe Paterno
Georgia	Hello, Hairy Dawg!	Aimee Aryal	Purdue	Hello, Purdue Pete!	Aimee Aryal
Georgia	How 'Bout Them Dawgs!	Vince Dooley	Rutgers	Hello, Scarlet Knight!	Aimee Aryal
Georgia Tech	Hello, Buzz!	Aimee Aryal	South Carolina	Hello, Cocky!	Aimee Aryal
Illinois	Let's Go, Illini!	Aimee Aryal	So. California	Hello, Tommy Trojan!	Aimee Aryal
Indiana	Let's Go, Hoosiers!	Aimee Aryal	Syracuse	Hello, Otto!	Aimee Aryal
Iowa	Hello, Herky!	Aimee Aryal	Tennessee	Hello, Smokey!	Aimee Aryal
Iowa State	Hello, Cy!	Amy DeLashmutt	Texas	Hello, Hook 'Em!	Aimee Aryal
James Madison	Hello, Duke Dog!	Aimee Aryal	Texas A & M	Howdy, Reveille!	Aimee Aryal
Kansas	Hello, Big Jay!	Aimee Aryal	UCLA	Hello, Joe Bruin!	Aimee Aryal
Kansas State	Hello, Willie!	Dan Walter	Virginia	Hello, CavMan!	Aimee Aryal
Kentucky	Hello, Wildcat!	Aimee Aryal	Virginia Tech	Hello, Hokie Bird!	Aimee Aryal
Louisiana State	Hello, Mike!	Aimee Aryal	Virginia Tech	Yea, It's Hokie Game Day!	Frank Beamer
Maryland	Hello, Testudo!	Aimee Aryal	Wake Forest	Hello, Demon Deacon!	Aimee Aryal
Michigan	Let's Go, Blue!	Aimee Aryal	West Virginia	Hello, Mountaineer!	Aimee Aryal
			Wisconsin	Hello, Bucky!	Aimee Aryal
NBA					
Dallas Mavericks	Let's Go, Mavs!	Mark Cuban			
Kentucky Derby					
Kentucky Derby	White Diamond Runs For The Roses	Aimee Aryal			

More great titles coming soon!